Red Eyed Rabbit

By Bakthi Ross

Published by Waxwing
Waxwing
PO Box 373
Morayfield 4506
Australia

ISBN   978 1 922220 49 3

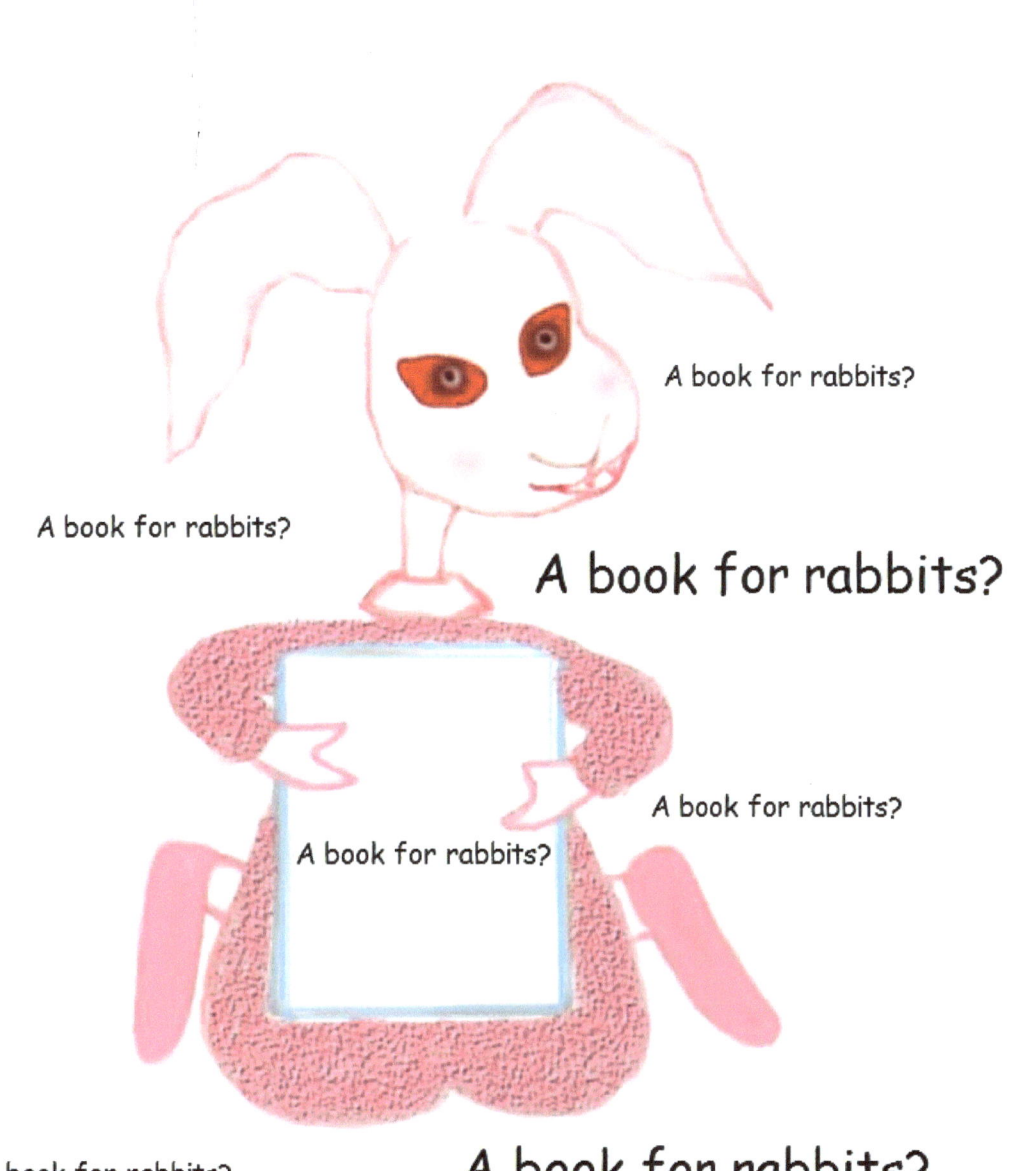

A book for rabbits?

A book for rabbits?

A book for rabbits?

A book for rabbits?

A book for rabbits?

A book for rabbits?

A book for rabbits?

Oh! Said the Red Eyed
Rabbit. A book for rabbits.

"I cannot read," said Red Eyed Rabbit.

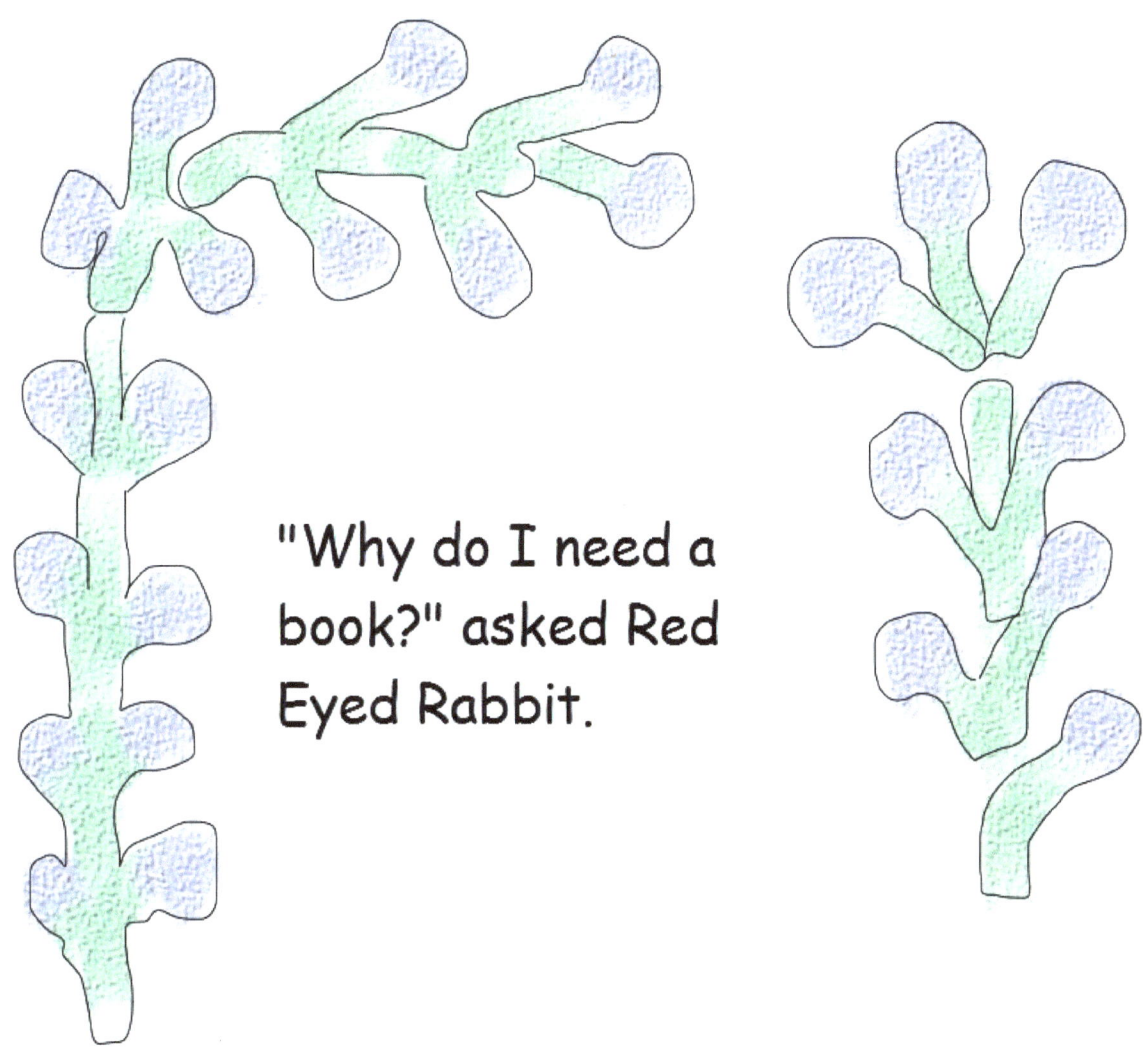

"Why do I need a book?" asked Red Eyed Rabbit.

"What a rabbit book would have?" said Red Eyed Rabbit.

It would have carrots and cabbages.

Cabbages!

A rabbit run.

A rabbit hop.

Two rabbit ears.

A twitching nose.

A rabbit sleep.

A big rabbit warren.

Red Eyed Rabbit looked at the book.

"Hey! I wrote a book for rabbits," said
Red Eyed Rabbit.

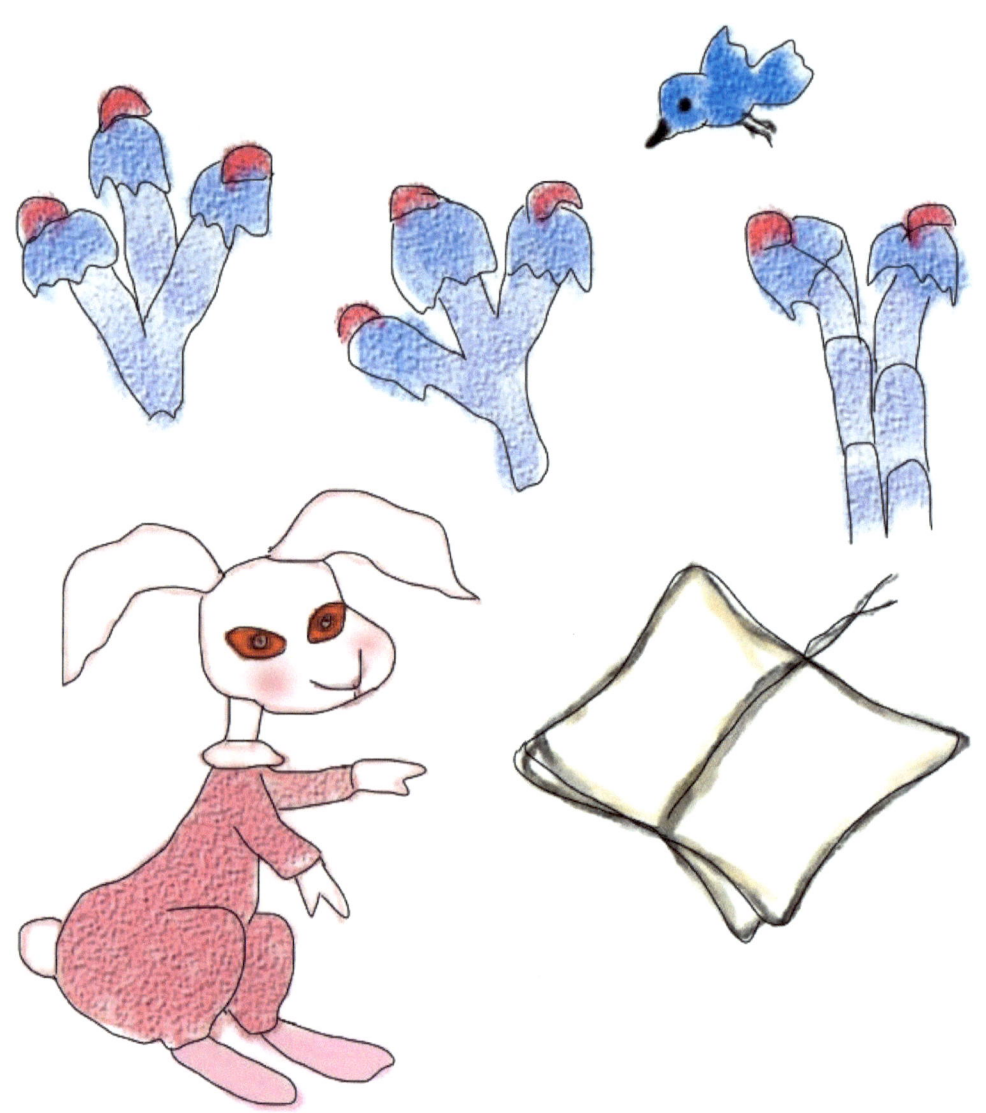

"Now I can read and write books," said Red Eyed Rabbit.

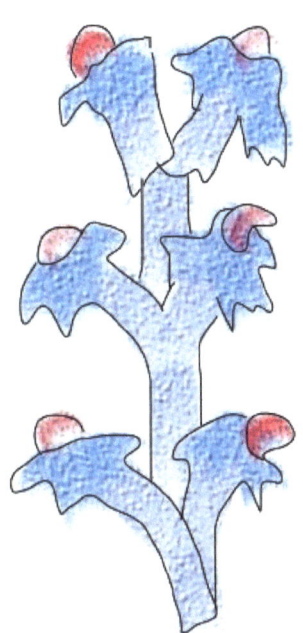

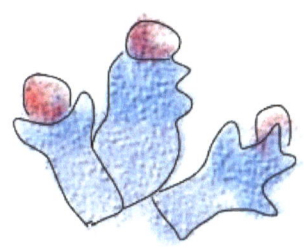